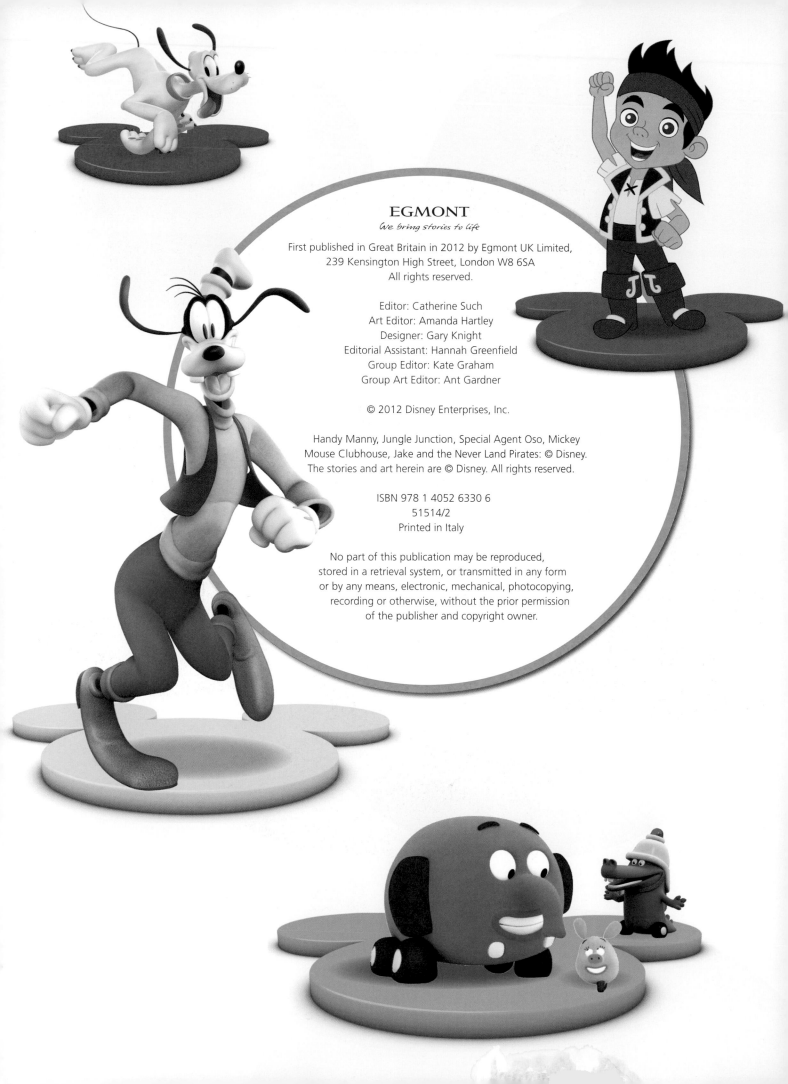

# EGMONT

*We bring stories to life*

First published in Great Britain in 2012 by Egmont UK Limited,
239 Kensington High Street, London W8 6SA
All rights reserved.

Editor: Catherine Such
Art Editor: Amanda Hartley
Designer: Gary Knight
Editorial Assistant: Hannah Greenfield
Group Editor: Kate Graham
Group Art Editor: Ant Gardner

© 2012 Disney Enterprises, Inc.

Handy Manny, Jungle Junction, Special Agent Oso, Mickey
Mouse Clubhouse, Jake and the Never Land Pirates: © Disney.
The stories and art herein are © Disney. All rights reserved.

ISBN 978 1 4052 6330 6
51514/2
Printed in Italy

# This annual belongs to

· · · · · · · · · · · · · · · · · · · · · · · · · · · · · · · · · · · · · · ·

**Write your name here.**

# All of this inside ...

### Mickey Mouse Clubhouse

### Jake and the Neverland Pirates

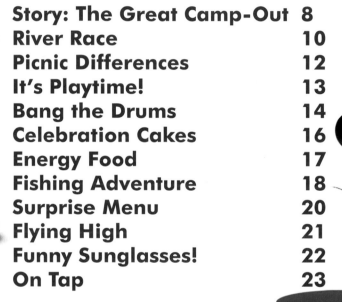
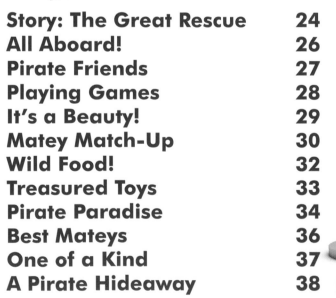

**1**

The friends were driving to the country,
To enjoy the outdoors in the sun.
They wanted to earn their Camp-Out Badge,
And have lots of camping fun!

**2**

"I'll make my **TENT**, over there!"
Donald had his own camping plan.
He didn't want to share and he knew,
There were only three tents in the van!

**Look at my TENT!**

**3**

So, Donald made a **TENT** for himself,
"I'll have more fun on my own!"
He used a blanket and a golf club,
To make his cosy new home.

**4**

Then it was time to go fishing,
And the water was deep and blue.
"What will we catch?" wondered Mickey,
"Hopefully a fish or two!"

**8**

**?** Can you **FIND** these
details in the story

# Camp-Out

**5**

**Oh no! The TENT!**

**6**

Donald wanted to fish alone,
He didn't think that was wrong.
He caught something straightaway,
But the fish was very strong!

The fish pulled the boat very fast,
And Donald ended up on the shore!
First, he ran into Goofy's TENT,
Then knocked down more and more!

**7**

**8**

Soon Donald's was the only TENT left,
So where would the others rest?
"You can share my TENT," Donald said,
"Camping with friends is best!"

They'd earned their Camp-Out badge,
And their trip had been lots of fun.
"Next, let's do our fishing badge,"
Laughed Mickey, to everyone!

# River Race

What do Mickey and Donald need to **TRAVEL** on the river? Now, **LEAD** them along the river to join Minnie and Daisy!

Answers on page 67.

11

# Picnic Differences

Answers on page 67.

Can you HELP Minnie FIND FIVE differences in the bottom picture? TRACE over a number each time you find one.

12

# It's Playtime!

Mickey wants to play with you! Can you COLOUR the picture? USE the number key to help you.

*

Help your child look for shapes in his own toys. Can he find a cube, a pyramid and a cylinder?

13

# Bang the Drums

**HELP Goofy play his drum kit by TRACING over the lines. SHOUT the sounds out loud as you reach them!**

CRASH!

CRASH!

CRASH!

THUMP!

THUMP!

THUMP!

TIPPY TAPPY!

TIPPY TAPPY!

TIPPY TAPPY!

BANG!

BANG!

BANG!

# Energy Food

Minnie needs lots of energy when she goes rollerskating. **COLOUR** the dotted areas to reveal an energy-giving food. Now, **TRACE** over her trail as she speeds off.

17

Answer on page 67.

# Fishing Adventure

Mickey and Donald are going on an exciting fishing adventure! How many of each coloured fish from the panel can you **COUNT** in the scene? Watch out for the mischievous whale!

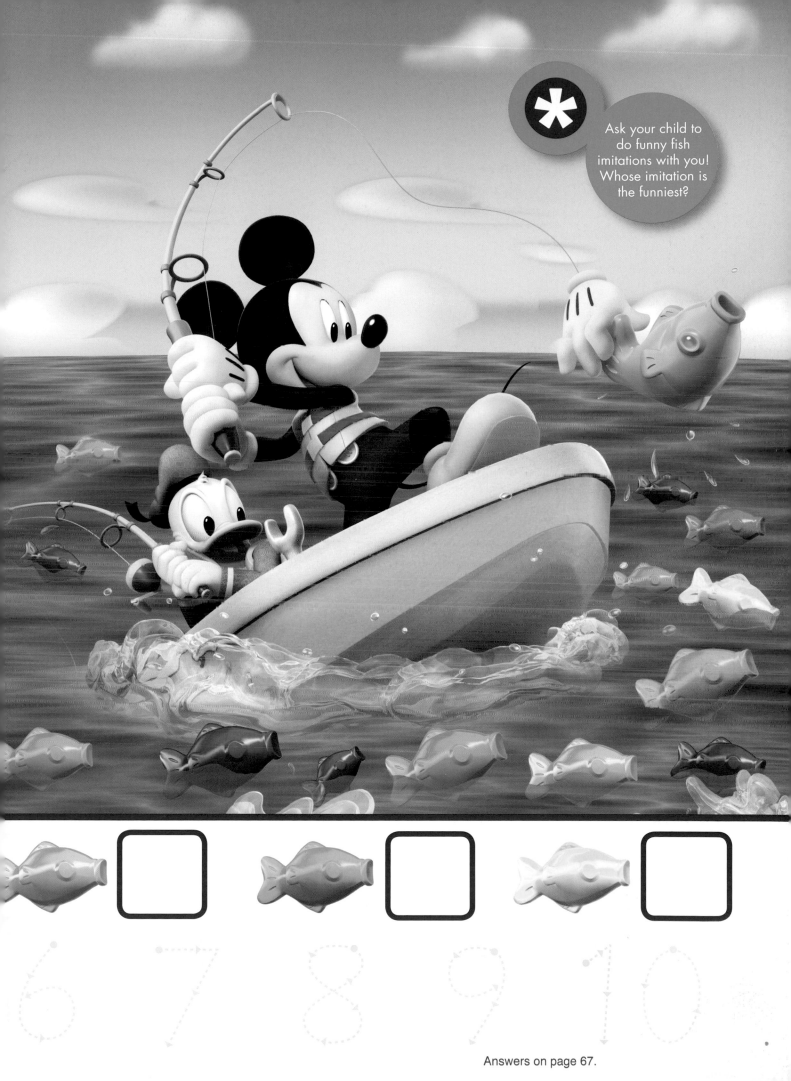

Answers on page 67.

# Surprise Menu

What is Goofy going to serve to each of his friends? FOLLOW the trails with your finger to find out!

Answers on page 67.

# Flying High

Mickey and Donald are flying high above the clouds in their big balloon. Look! They have spotted a rainbow! Can you ADD some bright colours to the picture?

# Funny Sunglasses!

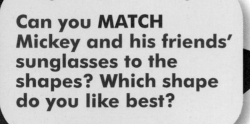

Can you MATCH Mickey and his friends' sunglasses to the shapes? Which shape do you like best?

**Square**

**Rectangle**

**Circle**

**Star**

Answers on page 67.

On Tap

Can you help Mickey put these glasses of water in ORDER, starting with the empty glass?

Hot dog!

a

b

c

d

Answers on page 67.

# The Great Rescue

**READ** this adventure story about a treasure chest. When you see a **PICTURE**, shout the word out loud.

It was an exciting day in Never Land. 🏴‍☠️ and his crew had found some treasure. "Look at all these 💎," cried 👧. They didn't know 🪝 was watching them.

At lunch, 🏴‍☠️ and his friends went off to get food, but when they returned, the treasure had gone! "🪝 must have stolen it!" said 🏴‍☠️. The crew marched off to the Jolly Roger boat.

When they arrived, 🪝 and his men were inspecting the treasure. "We need a plan!" said 🏴‍☠️. 👧 had the perfect idea. She found a little ticking clock and hid behind some nearby rocks.

"What's that?" shouted . He rushed to the front of the boat. TICK TOCK, TICK TOCK! "It must be the Tic Toc Croc!" shouted Mr. Smee.

Whilst and his men were distracted, and Cubby tiptoed onto the boat to get the treasure back. "Quick!" cried , as the started to clink together.

Before had time to chase after them, the crew grabbed the treasure and ran off along the beach. "We fooled you again!" cheered, happily. It was another successful rescue for and his crew!

**THE END**

25

# All Aboard!

Jake loves to explore different pirate ships. Can you help him put these ships in order of SIZE, starting with the SMALLEST?

Can you SPOT Captain Hook hiding on one of the boats?

SMALLEST

BIGGEST

# Pirate Friends

Jake and his friends are throwing Skully a birthday party, but ... surprise! There are FIVE differences between these two pictures! Can you FIND them all?

**Tick a circle as you SPOT each difference.**

27

Answers on page 67.

# Playing Games

Jake and his friends have been playing with their toys all morning! HOW MANY of each type have they brought onto the beach?

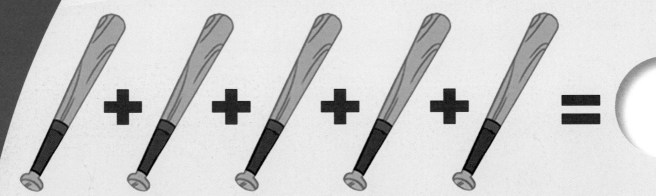

🏏 + 🏏 + 🏏 + 🏏 + 🏏 = ◯

⚽ + ⚽ + ⚽ + ⚽ + ⚽ = ◯

🛹 + 🛹 + 🛹 = ◯

**Use the number line to help you.**

28 | 1 2 3 4 5 6 7 8 9

Answers on page 67.

# It's a Beauty!

Jake loves the swashbuckling natural beauty of Never Land! Have fun COLOURING him and his animal friend, using the dots as a guide!

# Matey Match-Up

Everyone knows that pirates hang out in crews and it's the same in Never Land. Can you MATCH the two crew leaders with the right shipmates? COLOUR the circles in BLUE for Jake's crew and RED for Hook's crew. We've done the first one for you.

Can you FIND the boot?

SKULLY

MR. SMEE

BONES

30

SHARKY    IZZY    CUBBY

**31**

Answers on page 67.

# Wild Food!

There's fruit and veg a-plenty in Never Land! Help Izzy, Cubby and Skully choose some party snacks by DRAWING the next item in each sequence.

Answers on page 67.

# Treasured Toys

Jake and Cubby love playing with outdoor toys. Do you know what they'd like to play with next? **COLOUR** the spaces marked with a black dot to find out if you're right!

**a**

**b**

33

Answers on page 67.

# Pirate Paradise

Jake and his friends are having a rest on Pirate Island! Can you FIND the objects below in the scene? TICK a box as you spot each one.

34

# Best Mateys

Jake, Izzy and Cubby are best mateys, and they're always working together on their never-ending adventures! Help complete the team picture by PUTTING the puzzle pieces in the right places!

b

c

a

d

1

2

3

4

Answers on page 68.

# One of a Kind

Captain Hook is trying to catch a butterfly, but which one does he want? Can you **SPOT** the only one that's **DIFFERENT** from the rest? That's the one he's after!

Now **COLOUR** Captain Hook.

Answer on page 68.

# A Pirate Hideaway

Mateys, look out! Jake and his crew are hiding from Captain Hook! How many of them can you FIND hiding in the scene?

Some toys have washed up on the beach. Can you NUMBER them from biggest to smallest?

38

Children love hiding. Playing hide-and-seek and finding the best hiding places at home is always so much fun.

39

**1**

Jungle Junction was very busy,
The big rain was coming today.
The friends had to collect water,
Before the dry season came to stay.

The water will roll down the **LEAF**!

**2**

Ellyvan was making a 'drip tip'.
"This will work without fail!
The rain will roll down the **LEAF**,
And collect in the pail."

**3**

But when Ellyvan tested the 'drip tip',
Something wasn't quite right.
The **LEAF** spilled the water on the ground,
It was a very funny sight!

**4**

Just then there was a shout,
From Crocker way up high.
"The big rain is coming!
Look at the raincloud in the sky."

**40**

**?**

Can you SPOT these details in the story?

# Invention

**5**

"But the 'drip tip' isn't ready,"
Ellyvan said sadly.
"I have an idea!" Dozer cried.
"Everybody come with me."

**6**

The plan was very simple,
Dozer told them what to do,
"We'll blow the raincloud far away!"
So everybody blew and blew!

I need to move the LEAF!

**7**

"Now I've got a bit more time,"
Said Ellyvan happily.
"If I move this LEAF a little,
The 'drip tip' will work for me."

**8**

When the raincloud came back,
And the big rain began to fall,
The 'drip tip' worked perfectly.
Ellyvan collected the most rain of all.

# Going Home

Answers on page 68.

After a fun day together, Bungo is helping the Beetlebugs find the best road home from the river. **FIND** the path with the **FEWEST** obstacles.

a

b

c

42

# Animals with Wheels

Can you tell that Zooter is both a piglet and a messenger bike, and that Hippobus is both a hippopotamus and a bus? Follow the colour key guide and **COLOUR** the two 'wheelers' to see for yourself.

1 =
2 =
3 =
4 =

43

# Shopping List

Zooter and Bungo are shopping. Can you help them by **COUNTING** the items they have bought, then tracing over the number next to each of the items?

Reinforce your child's number skills, by counting different items around the house.

44

Answers on page 68.

# Sports Day

It's sports day in Jungle Junction and the Jungle gang are having lots of fun. Join in by **TRACING** over the track below as fast as you can, to reach the finish.

**START**

Zooter won a red rosette for coming first. Can you COLOUR this rosette in your favourite colours?

FINISH

**1**

On the morning of Manny's birthday,
The **TOOLS** decorated the shop.
"One last streamer," Dusty cried out,
"Before it's time to stop!"

**2**

The gang had only just finished,
When Manny came through the door.
"Wow!" he cried. "What a surprise!
I couldn't have wished for more!"

**3**

"Happy birthday!" sang the **TOOLS**,
As loudly as they could.
"Now, let's get the party started!"
They knew it was going to be good!

**4**

The **TOOLS** led Manny to the piñata,
A hanging star filled with sweets.
He put on a blindfold and used a stick,
To break it to reach the treats!

**48**

Can you SPOT these
details in the story?

**5** Manny's first swing hit the piñata,
And the sweets came tumbling out.
"Hooray!" cried Manny, with a grin,
He had given it quite a clout!

Come on, Tools!

**6** "That one's mine!" Rusty cried,
Grabbing a sweet with one bite.
The **TOOLS** were very excited,
They'd never seen such a sight!

**7** At that moment, a voice called out,
"Where's the birthday boy?"
Kind-hearted Kelly had baked a cake,
And she carried it in, full of joy.

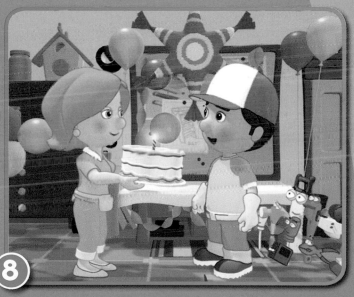

**8** "Thank you, Kelly!" said Manny, happily,
"I'm pleased you could be here."
He blew out the candle, making a wish,
To have fun, every day of the year!

# Odd One Out

Manny is packing things that you can use to communicate: a radio, a television, a microphone and a camera. Help Manny SPOT the odd one out in each row.

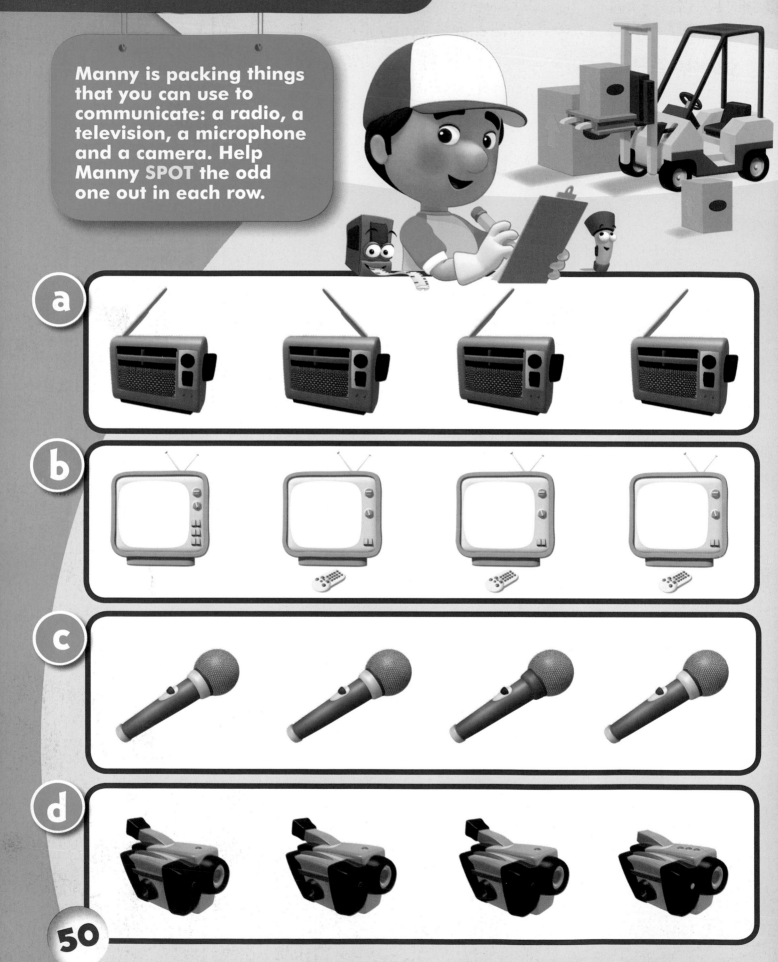

# Football Fun

Manny and the Tools are playing football in the park. **COLOUR** this happy picture.

51

# Manny's Day Off

Manny and the Tools are enjoying a day off! Can you **GUIDE** them through the maze to meet Kelly and Abuelito, passing each of the fun activities on the way?

**Start**

52

Finish

Answer on page 68.

# Tool Playtime!

Manny is fixing the swings at the park. Can you COUNT the objects in the scene?

Write the correct number of each of the objects in the boxes below.

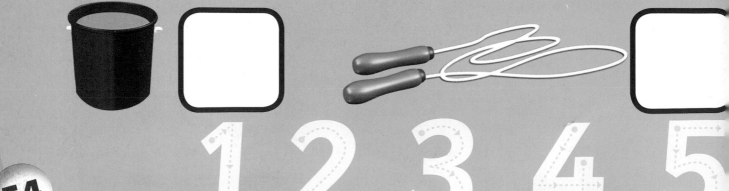

54

6 7 8 9 10

Answers on page 68.

# Carnival Flags

Manny is hanging flags for a street carnival. COLOUR the flags in each row to COMPLETE the sequences!

a

b

c

d

Answers on page 68.

# Play with Fix-It

Manny is playing
a ball game with Fix-It.
Find your brightest pens
to COLOUR the scene.

**1**

One day at the nursery school,
Sam was feeling a little blue.
He needed a partner for a nature walk,
And didn't know what to do.

**2**

But Sam didn't need to worry,
Agent Oso was on his way.
He would help Sam find a friend,
Agent Oso would save the day!

DON'T WORRY, SAM!

**3**

Sam couldn't believe his eyes,
When Oso walked through the door.
"We need to follow 3 special steps!
Now let me tell you more."

01

**4**

Step 1 was to choose a friend,
They spotted a small BOY.
He was in the sandpit by himself,
Playing with a colourful toy.

**?**

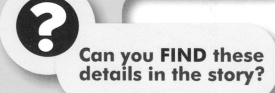

Can you **FIND** these details in the story?

# Friend

**5** Step 2 was to introduce himself,
Agent Oso was standing by.
He watched Sam walk up to the BOY,
Introduce himself and say "hi".

**6** Then it was time for step 3,
Invite the BOY to play.
"Would you like a go with my truck?"
Agent Oso heard Sam say.

**7** It was nearly time for the nature walk,
Sam had one more thing to do.
He asked the BOY to be his partner,
The BOY said: "Yes, I'll come with you."

**8** Sam thanked Agent Oso,
Now his mission was at its end.
It had been a great success,
And Sam had a brand new friend.

# Toothbrush Time

Agent Oso is brushing his teeth before bed. Can you **FIND** the missing piece of the puzzle?

\* Ask your child what other preparations are made before going to bed, like changing into his pyjamas.

a

b

c

Answer on page 68.

# On Top of the World!

It's time for a training exercise in the mountains with Special Agent Wolfie! Put the THREE steps in the right order to help Oso climb up the mountain! The first has been done for you.

Once you've helped Agent Oso reach the top, have fun COLOURING him in!

1

63

Answers on page 68.

# Sea Creatures

Agent Oso is exploring underwater. Help him **FIND** the octopus, then **COLOUR** it in!

TRACE the word octopus.

octopus

How many of each different coloured fish can you COUNT? WRITE the numbers in the boxes.

Answers on page 68.

# Flying Fun

Oso and his friends are flying their kites! Can you **FIND FIVE** differences in the bottom picture? **TRACE** a number each time you find a difference.

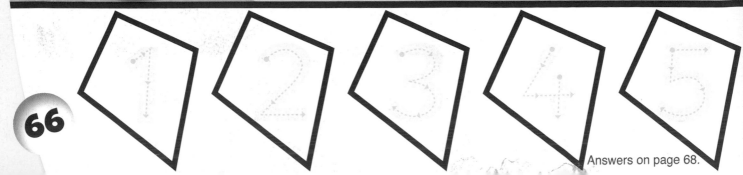

**66**

Answers on page 68.

# Answers

## Pages 10-11
### River Race
Donald and Mickey need the boat to travel on the river.

## Page 12
### Picnic Differences

## Page 16
### Celebration Cakes
a and f, b and i, c and g, d and h. Both e and j are not part of a pair.

## Page 17
### Energy Food
The dotted areas reveal a bunch of bananas.

## Pages 18-19
### Fishing Adventure
Purple – 2, blue – 6, red – 9, green – 5, pink – 2, yellow – 3.

## Page 20
### Surprise Menu
Mickey – hamburger, Daisy – soup, Donald – cupcake.

## Page 22
### Funny Sunglasses!
Mickey – circle, Donald – star, Minnie – rectangle, Goofy – square.

## Page 23
### On Tap
c, a, d, b.

## Page 26
### All Aboard!
2, 1, 3, 4.
Captain Hook is hiding on boat 4.

## Page 27
### Pirate Friends

## Page 28
### Playing Games
Baseball bats = 5, footballs = 5, skateboards = 3.

## Pages 30-31
### Matey Match-Up
Jake's shipmates: Skully, Izzy, Cubby.
Hook's shipmates: Mr. Smee, Bones, Sharky.
The boot is on the rocks near Captain Hook.

## Page 32
### Wild Food!
a. Apple.
b. Orange.
c. Banana.

## Page 33
### Treasured Toys
a. Rugby ball.
b. Boomerang.

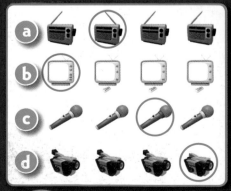